D0756571

THE LONDON BOROUGH
www.bromley.gov.uk

PETTS WOOD
01689 821607

Please return/renew this item
by the last date shown.
Books may also be renewed by
phone and Internet.

ReadZone Books Limited

© in this edition 2015 ReadZone Books Limited
www.ReadZoneBooks.com

This print edition published in cooperation with Fiction Express, who first published this title in weekly instalments as an interactive e-book.

FICTI●N EXPRESS

Fiction Express
First Floor Office, 2 College Street,
Ludlow, Shropshire SY8 1AN
www.fictionexpress.co.uk

Find out more about Fiction Express on pages 106–107.

Design: Laura Durman
Page Layout: sprout.uk.com
Cover Image: Shutterstock Images
Printed in Malta by Melita Press

© in the text 2015 Bea Davenport
The moral right of the author has been asserted.

ISBN 978-1-78322-539-2

My Cousin Faustina

Bea Davenport

What do other readers think?

Here are some comments left on the Fiction Express blog about this book:

"Your story is absolutely AMAZING!!!. You are an extremely talented author and the way you left us with that suspense at the end was great. I hope everyone else has enjoyed this [book] as much as I have."
Grace, student blogger, Hackney, London

"I could not stop thinking about your amazing book My Cousin Faustina. *I LOVE IT. :)"*
India, student blogger, High Wycombe

"I really, REALLY like My Cousin Faustina! *Please write another book, telling us what happened next!"*
Kim, student blogger, Bishop Henderson CE VA Primary School, Taunton

"I REALLY LIKED My Cousin Faustina... *This book gives me the chills!"*
James, student blogger, Birmingham

"We are loving this story because it is very mysterious. It is very exciting because it is scary and spooky. We really want to find out what is going to happen to Faustina!"
Birch class, Ludlow Junior School

Contents

Thanks to all the team at Fiction Express
and to all the readers who helped shape this story

Chapter 1

A Surprise Guest

"See you tomorrow, mate," said Edson, giving me a playful punch on the shoulder. "Wow, Jez. What an awesome day, eh?"

It certainly was. I looked up at the school minibus as it trundled away, my mates giving me the thumbs-up from the back window.

Ever had one of those days when everything goes right? I just had.

I breezed through my history test in the morning, even though it was my worst subject.

I found a pound coin in the bottom of my school bag at lunchtime, a bit sticky but good enough to buy a can of cola and some sweets.

Our teacher Mr Fairclough – who we all call Floorcloth, on account of his habit of spitting as he talks then wiping it up with the corner of his sleeve – gave me an A for my geography homework.

And even better I scored three goals in the semi-final of the inter-schools cup. I won the 'Player of the Day' trophy and our headteacher told me I was a superstar. We were sure to win the league now, no question.

Was I a hero, or *what*?

I was actually humming to myself as I rounded the corner to my house. This day is getting better and better, I thought. Mum and Dad will probably treat me to fish and chips when I tell them the good news – I'm *starving*. This might be a great time to ask for that new game I've been after.

But then something strange happened.

As I opened the garden gate, a shadow passed over the sky. Looking up, I saw a huge swirl of black crows flying and screeching above me. They sounded as if they were laughing.

I stopped to stare for a moment as they circled – and settled on our roof, cackling and shuffling about as if they were getting ready to watch a show.

Weird, I thought as I shrugged and put my key in the door.

I was surprised to hear voices coming from the kitchen and I curled my lip as I trailed down the hallway. An unexpected visitor. The last thing I wanted was to have to be polite to some aged relative or boring neighbour.

Only it wasn't either of those.

Sitting at the kitchen table was a girl, about my own age. And my mum and dad were staring at her, with weird fixed grins on their faces.

The girl looked at me and blinked twice, very slowly. She had large, bright eyes – one an unnatural, electric blue and the other deep brown. Her hair was glossy black, and locks of it curled around her shoulders like fat snakes. "You must be Jez!" she purred.

Mum and Dad seemed to snap out of a trance.

"There you are," said Mum, crossly. "We thought you'd got lost. Trust you to be late home today of all days."

"Why? What's special about today?" I edged towards the table, where a selection of biscuits was neatly arranged on a plate. "I told you there was a match – it's *Wednesday*!"

"And *I* told *you* that your cousin was coming to stay. That's more important than football, our kid!" Mum swiped the plate away as I reached for a chocolate digestive, and tutted.

"More important than football? Even when I'm Player of the Day?" I grinned at Dad, expecting him to jump up and pat me on the back. But he just shook his head at me. "Anyway," I huffed, "you never mentioned a cousin…. I didn't even know I had one."

"I'm more of a second cousin," said the girl, in a treacly sort of a voice. "Or is it third? I can never remember."

She giggled and my usually sensible mother guffawed along with her while Dad gave her a simpering smile.

I looked from them to the girl and back again. What *was* going on here?

Chapter 2

Meet Faustina

"I'm Faustina." The girl stood up and held out her hand.

I didn't take it. "Faustina? That's… unusual," I replied.

"Old family name," she said, still holding out her hand.

"And what side of the family is that?" I folded my arms.

"Jez!" Mum snapped at me. "Shake hands with your cousin!"

Shake hands? Who was she, the *queen*?

Dad prodded me in the back, hard.

So I took the tips of Faustina's fingers in the very ends of my own for a tiny fraction of a second – enough to feel a strange, cold tingling sensation that ran all the way up to my elbow. I dropped her hand fast and stepped back. She gave me a bit of an odd look too, raising an eyebrow above her eerie blue eye. Had she had the same, electric-shock-style jolt?

"How… how long are you staying?" I asked, still startled.

Faustina batted her long lashes at me. "I'm not sure. Why do you ask, don't you want me here?"

I wanted to say, *"No, get out, you make my skin crawl as if I'm in a bath of maggots"*. But without even looking, I could feel Mum's angry eyes piercing the back of my head. I shrugged. "Just asking–"

"Well *don't*. It's rude," snapped Mum. "Faustina's mother is unwell, and we are her only family. So she can stay here as long as she likes."

She turned and gave Faustina a soppy look. "It's a pleasure to have you here, dear. And you really don't have to cook for us toni–"

"No, I insist," the girl interrupted, her voice smooth like silk. "It's the least I can do to say 'thank you'."

"Oh, well that's lovely," said Mum. "Really, really lovely." I could tell she was grinning from ear to ear.

Remembering I was starving, I peered over Mum's shoulder to see where she'd put the plate of biscuits. "What're you making, then?" I asked, glancing at Faustina.

"A traditional recipe, handed down through my family for many years," she replied. "It's a special kind of… of *stew*."

Urgh, I hate stew! So much for fish and chips.

I caught Faustina smirking at me. It was almost as if she knew what I was thinking. But of course, she couldn't possibly… could she?

"Jez," barked Mum. "Before you eat you must go and change out of your dirty kit."

"Yes, you do smell, just a little," Faustina sniggered.

To my disgust my mother laughed as well. "Yes, he does, doesn't he?"

"*He's* still here, you know," I reminded her.

"Yes," said Faustina icily. "Why is that?"

I glared at her, turned around and stamped out of the kitchen. Behind me, the door slammed of its own accord and with a horrible crash, the little panes of coloured glass fell out and shattered to a million pieces.

I turned and stared, my mouth open.

"Jez!" Mum shrieked. "Look what you've done!"

"You need to control that temper, boy," said Dad. "You'll have to pay for this out of your pocket money."

"But I didn't…." As I stared around at them, I could see there was no point in trying to tell them I hadn't touched the door.

Faustina was already on her hands and knees with a dustpan and brush. She looked up and gave me a sly look through her long eyelashes.

I slunk away.

* * *

Later, I was allowed back into the kitchen where Faustina plonked a foul-smelling bowl of gunge in front of me and said, "Enjoy."

Mum and Dad were already tucking

into their food, as enthusiastically as if they hadn't eaten for a week. How could they? It looked disgusting. Mum was murmuring about tomatoes and herbs and how she would have to get the recipe.

I stared into the bowl, which was full of an unidentifiable mess of slithery meat. It smelled like rotten eggs… and… wait… did something just move in there?

No, of course not, I told myself.

"Eat up, Jez," said Mum, actually licking her lips.

I tried one mouthful – horrible – put down my fork and said, "I'm not hungry." This was about the biggest lie I'd told all year.

"You're missing a real treat," said Dad, his voice thick with food. "Nowt wrong with this, lad. I'll have yours if you don't want it."

What had got into them? There was *so*

much wrong with this I didn't know where to start.

I shrugged and pushed the bowl in Dad's direction. Within minutes they'd gulped down the entire meal.

I looked up to see Faustina frowning at me, her mismatched eyes narrowed. She looked away instantly.

"I'm going to my room to do homework," I huffed.

"Er, you're in the spare room now, dear," chirped Mum.

"Wh-what?" I gasped.

"Well, we've put Faustina in your bedroom, Jez," said Dad. "You don't mind do you, son? We moved all your stuff out earlier."

"Thanks Jez," smirked Faustina. "It's really *kind* of you."

As I headed for the hallway I heard

Faustina offering to wash the dishes –
the little creep. Mum yelled "Listen to
that, our Jez. You could take a leaf out
of her book!"

Reaching the top of the stairs, I stopped
and listened. Then I quietly pushed open
the door to my bedroom – my *real*
bedroom – and peeped inside.

The first thing that hit me was that smell
again. Rotten eggs. I pinched my nose and
tried to breathe through my mouth. I
couldn't believe my eyes – all my football
posters were gone, my books, my games
console. Only my desk, my bed and an
empty bookcase remained.

A fat crow was perched on the
windowsill, looking at me with one beady
eye. On the bed, I could see a large, red,
leathery bag with weird writing on it.

Downstairs Faustina was still clattering

the plates around, so I crept into the room and tried to open the bag. The catch was a tricky one and, just as I got it open, I heard light footsteps coming up the stairs. It wasn't Mum or Dad. It had to be Faustina and she was about to find me rifling through her belongings….

Chapter 3

Evil Eyes

I heard the eerily faint footsteps reach the landing. My heart pounding, I rifled inside the leathery old bag, grabbing the first thing that met my fingers. It felt like a wodge of thick, folded paper. As the bedroom door opened, I pushed it into my back pocket and whipped round to see Faustina standing in the doorway.

"You're in the wrong bedroom, Jez." Her voice was like melted ice cream – soft but very cold. "This one's mine now, remember?"

She looked at her bag and back to me. "Have you been going through my things?"

I held up both hands and shook my head. "I just thought I might have left my… er… phone in here." I could feel Faustina's odd, bright eyes boring into me like needles.

"There's *nothing* of yours left here, so… you can *leave*." Faustina stepped aside from the door, glaring at me.

"I was going anyway," I said as I stomped through the door, slamming it behind me… and bumping straight into Mum. She stood on the landing, her arms folded.

"What are you doing in Faustina's room?" Mum snapped. "You'd better not be upsetting her, Jez."

A strange whimpering sound came from behind the bedroom door. Mum strode past me and pushed it open. "What on earth…?"

I stared into my – now Faustina's – room. It looked as if there had been a small explosion. Clothes and bedding were strewn all over the floor and, along the wall, in big, bold letters, were the words 'GO HOME'.

I felt my mouth fall open.

Faustina wiped a tear from her face. "I don't want to get Jez into more trouble," she sniffed. "But…." She waved a hand over the terrible scene.

Mum turned round slowly to face me. I'd never seen her look so angry. Her brow was furrowed like a newly-ploughed field!

"Now, wait a minute," I gasped, my face burning.

"I'm *ashamed* of you, our Jez," Mum shouted. "How could you *do* this to your lovely cousin?"

"Third cousin,' I pointed out. "And I–"

"You'll spend your weekend painting that wall," Mum interrupted. "Just you wait till I tell your father. Apologize to Faustina this minute!"

"But…." I started.

"*Jeremy*!" Mum barked. I knew what that meant – she hadn't called me 'Jeremy' for years, but it had never been a word to argue with.

"Sorry, Faustina," I mumbled, sounding as un-sorry as I dared.

"That's all right," said Faustina, her mouth stretching into a wide grin that reminded me of a baby alligator I once saw at the zoo. "You know, I only want to be friends."

I gritted my teeth and narrowed my eyes.

Mum pushed past me. "Go to your room, Jez. I've had enough of this behaviour. I don't want to see you again tonight."

"Fine," I said, tramping over to the little box room. Inside, there was barely any space to turn around. All my things were piled up untidily in a corner, and my posters lay crumpled on top of the bed.

How had Faustina done it? In the space of a few hours, she'd got me kicked out of my room, made Mum angry with me, and managed to frame me for two things I didn't do. And that was another mystery – she'd only been in the room by herself for a few seconds. How had she created all that chaos?

I yanked the papers I'd found in Faustina's bag out of my pocket. One piece fluttered to the floor. The other was crinkly, brown and old – and covered in scrawled words and symbols that I couldn't understand.

Peering at it, I turned it around to see if it made more sense upside down. It didn't.

I ran my finger along two words at the top and mouthed them aloud: *Cham-e-lia ven-if-ica.* What on earth did that mean? There were drawings on the page too – black-winged birds, stars and moons and all sorts of other things.

I picked up the other piece from the floor and stared at it. I knew what that was, all right – it was a map of the town. My street, my house and my school were all marked on it in shiny red ink.

Checking the bedroom door was firmly shut, I eased open my laptop. Carefully I typed in the words *Chamelia venifica.*

'Do you mean Chameleon?' asked the search engine.

"No, I don't," I muttered, tapping at the buttons again and adding double quote marks around the phrase.

Then something pinged up. The exact words: *Chamelia venifica* were mentioned on a site called 'Ancient and Extinct'. I clicked on the link and started to read: 'Little is known about these magical creatures – but they are powerful and dangerous….'

A rap at the door made me jump and I slammed down the lid of my laptop, stuffing the papers underneath my pillow.

Dad came in. "I knew it," he said. "This is no punishment if you're just sitting here playing games. I'll take that computer for tonight, thank you."

"I wasn't playing games," I protested. "I was… it was homework."

I think he knew I was fibbing. Without another word, he picked up my laptop and headed for the door. "You can have it back when you learn how to behave."

I put my head in my hands. I would find out who Faustina really was, I promised myself. But it wouldn't be tonight.

Chapter 4

Entranced!

I managed to avoid Faustina for most of
the next day at school, until I went into
the history classroom for our final lesson.
As I headed over to sit beside Edson,
Faustina appeared, pushing between us
and introducing herself as my cousin. I
rolled my eyes at my best friend, but he
didn't seem to notice.

Then Miss Bane – everyone's least
favourite teacher – marched into the
classroom and banged on the desk to get
everyone to stop talking. She peered at

Faustina. "Are you in the right class, young lady?"

Faustina stood up. "Oh, yes," she said, in the sugary simper that set my teeth on edge. "Definitely. I'm new to the school, but history is my favourite subject so I am very much looking forward to your lesson, Miss Bane."

Honestly, could Faustina be any creepier? I turned to Edson and pretended to put my fingers down my throat... but again Edson didn't notice – in fact he was smiling, dreamily, at Faustina.

"That *is* nice to hear," Miss Bane said, her perfectly plucked eyebrows raised. "Thank you, er–" She glanced at the register. "Oh, Faustina? What an unusual name."

"It's a very old Italian name. Medieval, in fact." Faustina's gleaming stare was fixed on Miss Bane. "I can speak some old

Italian," Faustina went on. "Would you like me to do that, Miss?"

Miss Bane just nodded, her eyes a little blank. I frowned at her and glanced back to Faustina. She started to say some words, very slowly and quietly, as if she was chanting a poem. I'd never heard any kind of language like that before.

The lights seemed to dim and I suddenly shivered, as if there'd been a fall in the temperature. Outside the window, a row of black crows had gathered along the goalposts as if they were watching… and listening. They shuffled together and cackled amongst themselves. Inside the classroom, everyone else had gone strangely quiet.

Miss Bane leaned forward and put her hand to her ear. "Speak up, Faustina. I can't quite hear you and I would very much like to learn a little medieval Italian."

Faustina's voice was low and sing-song. The words sounded like, *Volisserum, tibrassimus, dedo…*. And Miss Bane repeated them after her, in just the same chanting way.

The room now felt bone-cold. Goosebumps crept up my arms and legs. As I stared around, it looked as if the whole class was mesmerized, apart from me. I had to distract them… but I couldn't think of anything to say. So, I did the first thing that came into my head: the loudest, longest burp I could muster. It certainly made everyone jump.

Edson was the first to burst out laughing and the whole class joined in. Faustina turned to me. Disappointingly, she didn't look annoyed. In fact, she smiled. The weirdest thing, though, was that Miss Bane didn't say a word. Usually, something like that would have got anyone into *big* trouble, but the teacher simply stood staring over everyone's heads, her mouth hanging slightly open.

It only took a moment for the class to realize that whatever was up with Miss Bane, they weren't going to get a history lesson that day. There was an eruption of noise – shouting and banging on desks.

I hissed at Faustina. "What did you do?"

Faustina smirked. "I don't know what you mean." She looked back at the teacher, who was smiling, but at no one in particular. Miss Bane didn't smile often, so her face looked very odd – as if an invisible hand was pushing her mouth into shape, but the smile hadn't reached her eyes. "Perhaps Miss Bane's not well," she said, innocently.

The classroom door burst open and Mr Fairclough stormed in. "What is this *din*, class..?" He stopped and looked at Miss Bane, who turned towards him with her new idiotic grin.

"We have a marvellous new pupil, Mr Fairclough," she squeaked. "Faustina has been teaching me some ancient Italian."

Floorcloth folded his arms. "That's very interesting, but can you please keep your class under control?" he bellowed, showering the floor with spit. "Perhaps Faustina could teach you the words for 'sit down and keep quiet'."

Out of the corner of my eye, I watched the crows fly away, like a black curtain lifting. Mr Fairclough would put Faustina back in her place, I was sure of it.

Meanwhile Miss Bane was walking, slowly and robotically, towards the door.

Her skin was a deathly white and her eyes looked as if someone had switched off the brain behind them. Her face had become hideously haggard… and she appeared strangely crooked as she walked.

Mr Fairclough watched the teacher leave, frowning. "Right, well, it seems that Miss Bane is unwell. Fortunately for you I have a free period, so I will take over the rest of this lesson," he announced. "Can anyone tell me what happened to Miss Bane?"

"Faustina did something," I blurted out, before I could stop myself. I got on well with Floorcloth, as a rule. I was sure he would listen to me. "I don't know what she did but it was something spooky – she sort of hypnotized Miss Bane or something."

"That's not true," shouted a voice…. It was *Edson's* voice. My *best* mate turned to me and hissed, "What're you on about, Jez? Faustina didn't do anything."

"No, she didn't," agreed some of the girls nearby.

Then everyone joined in.

"Jez is lying."

"You fibber!"

"Don't be so mean!"

Faustina spoke, silencing the others. "Why are you picking on me like this, Jez?" Tears welled up in her eyes, though the gloating stare behind them told me she wasn't really upset.

"Don't worry dear," said Floorcloth in a strange voice I'd never heard him use before. "I'll deal with this," he turned to glare at me. "I must say I am *shocked,* Jeremy," he continued, shaking his head. "Making up stories about your own cousin. And on her first day here at school."

"But it's true… what I said!" I looked wildly round at my classmates. "Faustina said some weird words and Miss Bane went all… zombie-like. Just look at her," I said, pointing to the corridor where Miss Bane was hovering, trance-like. "She's a hideous mess! Can't any of you see it?"

My classmates shook their heads, robotically.

"How *dare* you talk about a teacher in that way?" barked Mr Fairclough. "You will stay behind after school and write out a hundred times: I must not make up nasty stories."

"But…." I'd never had a detention from Mr Fairclough before.

"A hundred and fifty times!"

"Listen," I floundered.

"*Two* hundred!" boomed Floorcloth.

"Jez, you're only making things worse," Faustina pointed out, her eyes wide with fake concern. I could see the trace of a smirk around her lips.

Sulkily I sank back in my chair. There was clearly no point in trying to change Floorcloth's mind. I had to admit it, Faustina had won... again.

As the class filed out to go home, Faustina turned to me. Putting her head on one side she gave me a sickly smile. "I'm sorry, Jez. You do seem to keep getting into trouble these days. You'll be late home again, and of course, you'll miss the lovely meal I'm cooking."

I swallowed hard, thinking of the hideous food she would be serving up for my parents.

As soon as the classroom door shut, I picked up a pen. It was hard to write lines with my head full of what had happened to Miss Bane, and visions of Faustina's stew. I began to write: *I must not make up nasty stories....*

My gaze drifted to the window, where I could see Edson walking towards the darkening school yard. And there was Faustina – strolling next to him. Edson seemed to be listening intently to whatever she was saying.

Suddenly, they stopped and Faustina fixed Edson with one of her eerie stares. Her head turned slightly towards the window and a wicked little smile crept across her face when she saw me watching. She was definitely up to something – no doubt about it! Whatever she'd done to Miss Bane was one thing – but I couldn't let her get her claws into my best friend!

I ran to the classroom door and pushed at the handle. I rattled the door as hard as I could. It wouldn't budge – Floorcloth had actually locked me in!

There was only one thing for it. I ran to the window and, after a bit of a struggle, managed to open it, pushing it wide and climbing out. Good job we were on the ground floor, I thought.

I sprinted over to where Faustina and Edson stood and barged between them.

"Whatever you're trying to do, stop it," I said, as loudly and firmly as I could manage.

A strange light came into Faustina's eyes as she fixed me with a stare.

I glared right back. "No way are you going to do your hypnotising thing on me!" I said.

"Fine then," she replied and, with a grin, she raised her arms and made a quick, fluttering gesture with her long white fingers.

Chapter 5

Faustina Revealed!

ZZZAAPPP!

Suddenly I was thrown backwards by the force of an electric jolt. I landed, with a smack, on the ground.

For a moment, I couldn't think straight. I sat up slowly, rubbing the back of my head. *Ouch!* Everything hurt and my brain was spinning. And that's when I saw Faustina – properly, I mean. As I blinked, trying to clear my dizziness, she hovered over me like a vulture. I'd always thought she was pale, but now her face looked ghostly and skull-like except for her hooked, pointed nose. Her hands resembled curved claws, with long nails as sharp as knives. And her black hair fluttered around her face just like crows' feathers. Everything was dark, except for a chilly light all around Faustina.

I was too scared to make a sound – my mouth opened and closed but no words came out. Then suddenly Edson burst out laughing and poked me with the toe of his shoe. "Get up, Jez, you idiot! What are you playing at?"

I glanced at my friend, and then back to Faustina. To my surprise, the darkness lifted and she was back to her usual self. I blinked hard, but standing in front of me was just an odd-eyed, slightly spooky-looking girl, instead of a terrifying apparition.

I staggered to my feet. "Wh– what just happened? You looked like a… like a…." I trailed off, unsure how to describe the vision.

Faustina's eyes went as small as pins. "I looked like a *what* exactly, Jez?"

"Well… like… something *awful*," I mumbled.

"Jez, just back off!" Edson snarled, his face an angry scowl. "What *is* your problem with Faustina? You're being totally out of order."

"I… she…" I floundered, taken aback by his reaction.

"Forget about it. Let's head home, Eddie." Faustina beckoned to him.

Ha! I thought. Now she's in trouble. If there's one thing Edson can't stand it's being called Eddie. The last time someone called him that he went off like a firework.

But… not today. Edson was trotting along beside Faustina with a goofy grin on his face. He looked like an overgrown puppy.

"Hey," I called after them, brushing myself down. "She just called you Eddie. Didn't you hear her?" I marched briskly to catch up with them.

"You don't mind do you, Eddie?" simpered Faustina.

"Of course not," Edson said. "*You* can call me anything you like, Faustina."

I made a sort of a growling noise in my throat. I was obviously too late – Faustina had bewitched him somehow. There was no way Edson would *ever* choose a girl over me. He was my best mate… or at least I thought so.

I trailed behind them, my hands curled into fists in my pockets.

* * *

As soon as I got into the house, Mum rounded on me. "I've heard all about you today, our Jez – playing up at school and getting a detention. I don't know what's got into you, I really don't."

Detention – the two hundred lines! I'd forgotten all about them. I'd have to do them tonight and give them to Mr Fairclough tomorrow. *Great*.

"Make yourself useful," Mum continued. "Go and get your muddy football kit from yesterday and put it in the washing machine."

"I've got to–" I started, but one look at Mum's face warned me not to argue.

As I loaded the machine, I spotted a basket on the floor with some of Mum's clothes in it. "Shall I put these in too?" I asked, hoping to put her in a better mood.

"Yes, please," sighed Mum.

I was about to switch the machine on when – "*Wait* !" – Faustina's voice rang across the room.

I turned around. "What?"

"I saw something sticking out of the pocket of your mum's jeans." Pushing me aside, Faustina put her hand into the washing machine and pulled out a little card. She held it up. "It's a scratch card – you'd better check it Aunty Katie." Faustina handed it to Mum. "You never know, it might be a winner!"

"Ooh, well, I sometimes treat myself to one of these," cooed Mum. "I didn't think I'd bought one this week. I must have forgotten to scratch it."

Mum started rubbing at the card. "I never win anything, though," she said, smiling. "It's all just a bit of fun."

Faustina's eyes were fixed on Mum's hands. The room seemed to blur a little, like a screen going out of focus.

Then Mum stopped and stared. She blinked a few times. "I don't believe it." She looked up. "I've WON! I've won a THOUSAND POUNDS!"

Dad made a choking noise over his tea and Mum started jumping up and down like a big daft kid.

"Wow! That's brilliant, Mum!" I chirped.

"Well, no thanks to *you*!" Mum snapped back. "If Faustina hadn't stopped you, you'd have put it through the wash!"

"Just think," said Faustina, her eyes all wide and sparkling. "It would have been *awful* to lose all that money."

"That's right," said Dad. "You should be more careful, Jez."

"Well you shouldn't have left it in your jeans in the first place," I pointed out to Mum.

"How *dare* you speak to your mother like that!" croaked Dad.

But Mum didn't notice. She rushed up to Faustina and gave her a tight hug. "You're a little star, that's what you are. Thank *goodness* you were here. I say we all go out for a pizza to celebrate."

"Yeah, sounds great!" I chipped in, thinking pizza would *definitely* be better than Faustina's cooking.

"You're not invited, lad," said Dad.

"What?"

"Your behaviour's been a disgrace since Faustina arrived," Dad continued. "You can stay at home and learn some manners."

"Quite right," said Mum. "There's a little bit of Faustina's lovely stew left over from yesterday. You can heat it up in the microwave."

"But Dad… Mum," I spluttered with disbelief.

"Oh, Aunty," Faustina interrupted. "Why not let Jez come along too?"

I stared at her. What was she up to *now*?

"Please," Faustina urged, turning to Dad and giving him a pleading look. "Jez has had a rotten day. Why don't we all go out together and have some fun – like a proper family?"

"Well," sighed Mum, "I suppose–"

"No thanks," I snapped. Whatever plan Faustina had, I did *not* want to be a part of it. "I've got homework to do. I don't want to get into more trouble at school, do I?"

Faustina's spidery brows knitted together in a frown. "Fine. I was just trying to be friends."

"So you say." I glared back, ignoring Mum tutting at me and Dad shaking his head.

I stomped up to my room feeling as if the whole world was turning against me. Was I going mad? Was I wrong about Faustina?

The image of her skeletal face and her talons swam into my mind.

No! I was the only person who had seen the *real* Faustina… I just needed to find a way to make everybody else see it, too.

As I reached the landing, I turned as Mum, Dad and Faustina entered the hallway and started putting on their coats, chatting excitedly.

"Bye then," I shouted down.

They all glared up at me as Dad opened the front door, then they turned and filed out into the front garden without another word. As the door swung shut, I spotted a crowd of crows launching into the air in front of them.

Chapter 6

The Truth

Tramping past my *real* bedroom, I headed into the box room and slammed the door. Fortunately, Dad had put my laptop back on my desk, so I booted it up and started to type '*Chamelia venifica*', my fingers shaking slightly as I clicked the keys.

The 'Ancient and Extinct' site popped up again. I started reading where I'd left off, at the words '…powerful and dangerous'.

The article had been posted by a professor of ancient mythology at an Australian university. He claimed to have uncovered a previously unknown myth about a magical creature named *Chamelia venifica*. He said *Chamelia venifica* meant 'magical shape-shifter'.

"Ha!" I said, out loud. I *knew* it.

'The myth,' the article went on, 'describes a creature with terrifying powers. It could make people see whatever it wanted them to – and it could bend people to its will. The professor had nicknamed this power a 'glamour spell'.'

A good description, I thought, of everything Faustina had done to my friends and family. What if the *Chamelia venifica* wasn't just a myth – a story made up long ago? Didn't myths always contain some kernel of truth – 'no smoke without fire' and all that?

I carried on reading, my heart pummelling inside my chest, harder and harder.

'It was believed that some people could resist the Chamelia's charms.'

"*How*?" I asked, through gritted teeth. But the article didn't say.

And then I saw something that chilled me to the core. At the very bottom of the webpage was a primitive sketch of a terrible creature. It was hard to decipher at first, as it was so faded. I peered closely at the screen. The sketch showed a bird-like figure with dark, feather-like hair and a skeletal face. I jumped back in my chair. This face was just like Faustina's. Not the strange girl who had wormed her way into my house and school and was charming everyone I knew – but the evil-looking apparition I had glimpsed when she knocked me over earlier today. If Faustina was a *Chamelia venifica* what was she doing here and what did she want?

I felt as if someone had dropped ice down my back. Shuddering, I snapped the laptop shut – I didn't want to look at that image any longer than I had to. Then I jumped to my feet. That terrible creature was with my unsuspecting Mum and Dad – eating pizza!

I grabbed my coat and ran out into the dark November night. I *had* to save them. Faustina might be turning them both into Chamelia venificas at this very moment! My feet pounded the ground until I arrived, panting, outside the restaurant. Stopping to gulp down some icy air, I pressed my face against the glass. There were Mum and Dad, on the far side of the restaurant, a candle flickering on the table between them. Mum was smiling and chatting, Dad was digging into his pizza – but where was Faustina? Nowhere to be seen!

For a fraction of a second I hoped she'd decided to go and work her nasty spells on some other poor family. But deep down, I knew she was still around. A faint scent of rotten eggs hung in the air, for a start.

The sudden sound of wings flapping made me jump. I looked up into the starless sky to see a black shape passing overheard. Starting, I realized it was a mass of crows flying in tight formation. They swirled across to the nearby graveyard, where they all settled in the spiny branches of the trees.

Thinking about it, those crows seemed to follow Faustina everywhere she went.

I climbed over the low wall of the graveyard and crept behind the gnarled trunk of a huge old yew tree. At first there was no sound except for the loud chattering of the crows. Then a harsh voice cut through the air.

"What do you want?"

Fearing I had been discovered, I peeked round the tree trunk, steadying myself against its scratchy bark. There she was – the real Faustina, a tall, nightmarish figure. But she wasn't looking at me – she was holding out her fingers like wintry twigs towards the crows who began to squawk back at her.

"Nonsense," Faustina snarled, silencing them. "I am in complete control and I will only get better with practice. The more pathetic humans I turn, the more powerful I'll become."

The crows chorused a high-pitched reply – it reminded me of Edson's trick of scraping his knife across his dinner plate to make everyone wince.

Anger bubbled inside my stomach as I thought of how Faustina had bewitched my best friend, my mum and my dad with her stupid 'glamour' spells.

Suddenly a terrible, shrieking laugh cut through the air. "Jez? Ha!" Faustina cried. "Don't you worry about *him*. He won't be a problem for much longer! I have a pla–"

Chapter 7

A Turn for the Worse

I never got to hear the end of Faustina's sentence because the night air was shattered by a bloodcurdling scream. The wordless, screeching, terror-filled sound sent the crows scattering rowdily into the black sky and made every single hair on my body stand on end. Without thinking, I turned and ran back to the restaurant, my heart jumping so hard I felt it would burst out of my chest. Petrifying as it was, I knew who was making that ear-splitting sound – it was my *mum*.

The place was in uproar. Mum was yelling at the waiter to get an ambulance. And there was my dad – sitting at the table, staring into space. His face was as white as the blank page of a book and his body looked strangely hunched and crooked.

"Dad?" I ran to him.

He turned and gazed at me with hollowed eyes. "What are you doing here?" he growled. "*You* weren't invited!" Dad was normally so laid back that his venomous tone took me by surprise.

"Are you OK?" I asked.

"No, no, he's not," yelped Mum. "He's not right at all, our Jez!"

"I've not been feeling myself this evening," murmured Dad. "But I don't know what your mother is flapping about. Screaming like that – I think she burst my eardrum."

"But you went all pale, and sweaty and… and…." Mum trailed off.

"With all the stress this son of mine has been causing lately, it's no surprise I'm feeling a little under the weather!" snapped Dad.

Suddenly the air around us seemed to darken as Dad turned and glared into my eyes. Only it wasn't quite Dad looking back at me. His nose looked more pointed, his eyes bright and hard, and his hair… well, Dad didn't have much hair but what he did have seemed to flutter briefly… almost like a bird's feathers?

Mum screamed again. Immediately the vision lifted and Dad's face looked pale and clammy, but otherwise normal.

"What *was* that?" screeched Mum, pointing at Dad. "Did you see that, Jez?"

"Umm… what exactly *did* you see, Mum?" I asked, looking from Dad to her and back again.

"Well, your father… he looked sort of… *different.*"

"Don't be so ridiculous, Katie!" yelled Dad.

"*Jon*," Mum gasped, taken aback. I'd never heard Dad speak sharply to my mum before… *ever!*

"I'm absolutely fi… fi… I'm fine," Dad stuttered and then, without warning, he collapsed on to the hard stone floor.

"Uncle!"

I turned to see Faustina dash across the restaurant. Crouching beside my father, she lifted his head and placed her black woollen scarf underneath it.

"Get away from him!" I snarled. "This is all your fault."

"Jeremy," barked Mum, "you heard your father. If this is anyone's fault, it's yours – all this worry and upset you've been causing. You've turned your father into a… into a…"

She paused and for a moment I thought she was going to say 'a terrifying monster'.

"…into a nervous wreck!" she finished, promptly bursting into tears. Faustina jumped up, flinging her arms around my mum.

"Oh Aunty, it will be all right… it will all be OK," she soothed.

At that moment, two paramedics burst into the restaurant and ran across to Dad. One placed a hand on his neck while the other shone a light in his eye.

"His pulse is racing," said the first.

"No reaction," said the other. Then he turned to Mum. "We need to take him straight to A&E. Will you be coming with us in the ambulance?"

"Y-yes," stuttered Mum.

"Great, then you can give us all his details on the way."

Within seconds, the paramedics had lifted Dad on to a stretcher and into the back of the ambulance.

"I want to come," I said, as Mum climbed in after them, but she turned and shook her head.

"There's not room for all of us, Jez. Walk your cousin home. I'll call as soon as I have any news."

My *cousin*. For a split second I had forgotten all about that creature.

Faustina was standing in the restaurant doorway, watching as the ambulance sped away, its blue lights flashing.

"What did you do to my dad?" I hissed at her.

"What are you talking about Jez? I didn't *do* anything," Faustina said, casually dismissing my accusation.

"Don't bother trying to deny it," I yelled at her. "I know all about you. I know what you are."

"Oh, really?" Faustina bared her teeth at me. "And what exactly *is* that?"

I really wanted to blurt out everything I knew – about the website, the visions, the crows… but something stopped me. Through Faustina's smug expression I could detect a trace of panic… of fear even. If I told Faustina everything I knew now, I wouldn't be able to continue my investigations in secret. She'd be watching my every move… or worse!

"Well, Jez?" Faustina prompted.

"You're a horrible, stupid girl," I blurted.

As I turned and started to march home, I heard Faustina snigger and mutter something under her breath. It sounded like, 'little do you know'!

Back in the box room, I threw on my headphones and started up a computer game. I half hoped that Faustina would be locked out of the house, but eventually I heard her bedroom door – well, *my* bedroom door – slam shut.

* * *

I was still awake a couple of hours later when my phone rang. It was *Mum*. She told me Dad was still 'under observation' by the doctors, who were completely baffled by his case.

"So, Mum, what actually happened in the restaurant?" I wanted to know.

Mum paused for a minute. "Is your cousin with you?"

"No, thank goodness," I said. "Why?"

"Oh, Jez, I'm not sure," Mum whimpered. "All I remember is that your Dad was telling Faustina about that research he's been doing into our Italian ancestors. You know how he goes on a bit. And then – I don't know how to describe it. Things went a little hazy. I think I must've had a dizzy spell because just for a second, Faustina looked very odd – like something out of a horror film. She said she was going to 'powder her nose' and just after she'd gone, your Dad took this funny turn… and suddenly, for a moment… he looked… *awful* too." Mum sighed. "Honestly, Jez, I must be losing my marbles."

"No, Mum, I don't think you are," I said reassuringly. "Listen, do you remember Dad saying anything odd?"

"Well, I wasn't really listening."

"This is important, Mum – did Faustina make Dad speak any words in old Italian?"

"Hmm," Mum said, and I could tell that she was thinking hard. "Now that you mention it… I think perhaps I do remember him blathering something sort of… Latin-sounding."

"Did Faustina say it first?"

"I'm not sure… he might have been repeating her words," she sighed again. "Jez, do you think Faustina had something to do with this?"

"Well…" I hesitated. I'd love to have shouted 'YES', but Mum always seemed so defensive of Faustina that I didn't dare.

"Because," she said slowly. "I'm starting to think there's something–"

The line went dead and, almost at the same moment, my bedroom door slowly opened. The rotten egg smell hit me before Faustina's face peered inside. She tried a smile, though it looked more like a sneer.

"Cup of tea, Jez?" she asked, innocently. Then, seeing the phone in my hand, she continued, "Oh, have you heard from Aunty?"

"Y-yes," I mumbled. "She said Dad's come round but he's under observation… and then we got cut off."

"Oh dear," said Faustina, sounding completely unfazed. "I'm sure she'll call back when she can. Tea?"

"No thanks," I replied, shuddering slightly at the thought of what Faustina might serve in a mug.

She left without another word.

Chapter 8

A Frightening Encounter

A week later, Dad was still in hospital. The doctors couldn't work out what was wrong, but I was fairly sure I had half an idea at least. I tried to get Mum to admit to her fears about Faustina, but every time I brought up the subject, my creepy cousin appeared from nowhere and Mum clammed up. I think she was scared – and after what happened to Dad, who could blame her? But every day, as I left for school with Faustina, she would tell me to 'take care our Jez'.

When I got to school, things were no better. There were hundreds of kids there but I might as well have been all on my own, as hardly anyone ever spoke to me.

Floorcloth had given me detention every day for a month as a punishment for climbing out of the window. Now every night he stood over me in the classroom making me write lines. Last night I had to scrawl out, 'I must not be jealous of my cousin' a hundred times. As *if*!

Then I lost one of the only things I still enjoyed. Miss Bane, who was looking worse by the day, kept me behind after a lesson making me late for football practice. When I finally showed up, coach told me I was off the team. I argued that I was their star striker, but he shouted that there was no 'I' in 'team' and he was sure they'd cope just fine without me.

To make matters worse, none of my teammates stood up for me. Most just carried on as if nothing had happened, and some even sniggered. They were still laughing as I trailed miserably back across the pitch and into the changing rooms.

And then there was Edson. At first he'd refused to have anything to do with me. Now, if he did speak to me, it was to say something horrible or to insult me. He had started hanging around with a gang of older boys at school. They were always pushing the younger kids around or picking on people. I really couldn't understand what Edson saw in them.

The only time he ever seemed to smile was when Faustina was around. Each time she called him Eddie it made me wince like fingernails down a blackboard. But his face would light up. He was completely under her wicked spell.

While I was totally isolated, Faustina had become the most popular girl in school. All the teachers loved her and everyone wanted to be her friend. It was as if the better things got for Faustina, the worse things got for me. Some days I even began to wonder whether I'd got it all wrong about her. But then the visions of her crow-like face, my dad's unconscious body and Miss Bane's blank smile swam before my eyes.

No, Faustina needed to be stopped… and I was the only one who could do it. I *had* to find a way.

* * *

One night Floorcloth made me stay on really late in detention. It was dark and cold as I left the school gates and headed home. As I turned into Walkers Alley, I heard a voice I recognized. It was Edson and, as usual, he was with his new crowd of mates.

"Hi Edson," I said, trying to be friendly – like old times.

"Well, look who it is," said Edson. "Jeremy no-friends."

The gang laughed. It reminded me of the cackling crows in the graveyard. I looked up and on top of the walls either side of the alley *were* crows – hundreds, thousands of them. Their glinting black eyes stared back at me.

"What you lookin' at, Jez?" asked one of the boys. "Hoping for a superhero to save you?"

"Save me from what?" I asked.

"This," replied the boy, as a fist landed in my stomach. I fell to the floor, winded, hearing the boys laughing again… or was it the crows… or both?

"Get up," a voice said, and I pushed myself to my feet, clutching my stomach and breathing hard. I glared at the gang in front of me. The clouds suddenly parted, and as the moonlight brightened, all the boys' faces seemed to change for a split second… haggard skin, pointed noses, feathers.

I blinked. The wind blew a cloud across the moon and the lads appeared back to normal. Did I imagine it? Was Faustina getting to me so much, I was seeing *Chamelia venifica* everywhere? Or – did that really happen?

I had a split second to weigh up my options as the gang advanced on me. Fight or flight?

Chapter 9

An Unexpected Saviour

Edson and his horrible mates surrounded me, edging closer.

The biggest boy loomed over me and sneered, "This is where you get what's coming to you." He raised his meaty fist.

The rest of the gang sniggered and the crows squawked as I panicked, wondering what to do.

Then, suddenly, everything fell silent. The boys stood stock still, glazed expressions replacing the ugly scowls that had been on their faces. Without a word they all stepped aside as one, clearing a path towards me.

A smell of rotten eggs hit me right away.

"What's going on here?" Faustina's voice cut through the air like a knife. She walked forward, a fiery light in her eyes. Then she turned to the boy who had just threatened me. "You, speak," she commanded.

"We were just… just talking… to Jez," mumbled the boy.

"We wanted to stop him giving you such a hard time, Faustina," Edson said, stepping forward. "We were going to teach him a lesson, once and for all."

"Well don't," snapped Faustina and Edson's face fell. He looked genuinely upset and I almost felt a bit sorry for him. "I can look after myself. I don't need *you* to stand up for me."

"Sorry Faustina," the gang mumbled as one.

"And besides," she said. "Jez is my cousin."

"So you *say*," I growled as I pushed past her and headed down the alley. True, Faustina had just saved me from a gang of bullies. But if she was expecting a 'thank you', she was going to have a long wait.

"Hey," Faustina yelled. "Don't you dare walk away from me!"

I yelped with surprise as the ground unexpectedly slid away beneath my feet. My ankle twisted painfully and I fell, hitting my head on the icy tarmac.

As everything faded to blackness around me, I heard Faustina say, "Jez, when *will* you learn that it is better to be my friend than my enemy?"

* * *

I forced my eyes open, my head pounding. Taking in my surroundings, I realized I was back home in the box room.

"He's come round," Mum announced, perching on the bed beside me. "Thank goodness for that. You had us worried for a minute then, our Jez. Why don't you sip this, love?" she soothed, handing me a glass of water. "And tell me, what on earth happened?"

I frowned, trying to think of the last thing I remembered. Some images flashed before my eyes – a dark alleyway, crows, Faustina, ice….

"Um… um… I'm not sure," I mumbled.

"I've already told you," Faustina said sharply.

"Yes I know, dear, but–"

"He slipped on some ice," Faustina continued, cutting Mum off. "I was out with some friends when we found Jez in a heap on the floor beside a large frozen puddle. Edson carried him home for me."

"Edson!" I sat up suddenly as a warped vision of Edson's crow-like face flashed before my eyes. Pain surged through my head and I fell back on to the sofa cushions. "What have you done to him?" I croaked.

"Lie still, Jez," Faustina crooned with mock concern. "I think you must have hit your head quite hard. You're talking nonsense. You need to get some rest."

"Yes," agreed Mum. "Yes, I think that's a good idea, our Jez. We'll leave you in peace. Try and get some sleep." She leaned forward, kissing me gently on the forehead. Then she followed Faustina out of the room.

* * *

The next morning, Mum insisted I take a day off school. That was fine with me – the last thing I wanted was to hear Faustina boasting about how she'd rescued me. And besides, my head was still banging and my ankle was swollen.

I lay on the sofa trying desperately to piece together the scene from last night. I suspected Faustina had been lying, but try as I might, I couldn't remember what had actually happened.

Frustrated, I grabbed my laptop. I clicked on to the 'Ancient and Extinct' website, deciding to check out the professor's article once more. I wanted to make sure there was nothing I'd missed.

There was that sentence again: 'It was believed that some people could resist the Chamelia's charms.' This time I noticed a strange blue symbol at the end of the line.

Hovering over it, I discovered it was a hyperlink. I couldn't believe I hadn't noticed it before.

I clicked and an information box popped up on the screen. The text read: 'Legend has it that in the nineteenth century, a *Chamelia venifica* fell in love with a beautiful Italian girl. Fooled by his glamour spells, the innocent young lady married the creature and bore his children, never realizing her husband's true identity. Some of the descendants of this old Italian family were said to bear a trace of Chamelia blood and to, therefore, be resistant to the Chamelias' charms.'

An old Italian family? Wasn't that just what Dad was chuntering on about before he had his 'turn'? I smacked my hand to my forehead, wishing I'd paid more attention when Dad talked about our family tree.

Lifting myself gingerly from the sofa, I hobbled over to the bookcase and pulled out one of Dad's albums containing old family photos. On the first page was a picture of a stout old lady in a hat made of feathers. Beneath it, Dad had written, 'Great Aunt Venetia'.

I slipped the sepia-brown photo from behind the shiny plastic film to get a better look at it. Turning it over, I noticed some writing on the back in a faded, old-fashioned, scrawl. There were some words I didn't recognize – but also some drawings and symbols that I definitely did. They were the same as the ones I'd seen on the parchment from Faustina's bag!

"What are you up to, Jez?" said a wheedling voice behind me.

Faustina! How long had she been there?

"You should be resting that ankle," she went on.

Secreting the photo into my pocket, I limped back to the sofa. "Thought you were at school," I muttered.

"Well, I was *really* worried about you, so they let me come home early to see how you are," Faustina smirked. "Especially as I've worked so hard towards tonight's school concert."

I frowned at her. "What concert?"

"It's a special event. The whole town's attending." Faustina gave me a wicked little smile. "Such a shame you'll have to miss it, because of your… *accident*."

"Like I care," I huffed. "I hate concerts."

Faustina said nothing but her grin widened and her eyes sparkled eerily.

Mum came in with a sandwich on a plate. "Here you go, Jez. I have to head off to the hospital to see your dad. This school concert is at very short notice – it means I won't be able to visit him this evening."

She left the room, Faustina following closely behind her. They were still talking as they made their way down the stairs. I hobbled over to the doorway and peered out, trying to catch what they were saying.

"I *really* appreciate you making the time to come and support me, Aunty Katie," Faustina was gushing. "It's going to be a great event. We're raising funds for the earthquake victims in Ancona. And I've spent all day teaching the whole school an old Italian song."

Something made my skin prickle, as if cold fingers were running up and down my arms and legs. I knew what *that* meant. Faustina had found a way to get every single teacher and pupil under her spell!

She carried on talking while Mum was putting her coat on. "We're going to put the words up on the screen so that the audience can join in, too," Faustina was beaming at Mum, looking really proud of herself. "The school governors will be there, the town councillers… even the mayor – all singing my song!"

"I want to come," I blurted out.

Mum stared up at me as if I'd gone mad. "I don't think so, Jez. You need to rest."

"And you *hate* concerts," Faustina snapped, eyeing me suspiciously.

"That's true," agreed Mum. "No you're to stay here in the warm, Jez. No arguments."

Chapter 10

The Concert

When Mum got back from the hospital, I tried again to convince her to let me go to the school concert. But she was having none of it.

After changing into some smart clothes, she headed for the car with Faustina. I waved through the window as they pulled away. Mum waved back, but my cousin just sneered at me.

I limped out into the hall, grimacing at the pain in my ankle, and pulled on my coat. I'd tried all afternoon to think of a plan, but I hadn't really come up with anything. I just knew I *had* to find a way to stop Faustina turning the whole town into hideous creatures like herself!

As I stepped out on to the street, a strong bitter wind hit me in the face like a giant snowball. My head throbbed, and my ankle ached as the cold penetrated my bones. I skidded on a patch of ice, managing to steady myself against our neighbour's garden wall.

Slowly and carefully, I made my way to school, my breath coming out in short, steamy little gasps and my heart galloping. I had to go the long way round as the thought of cutting through Walkers Alley gave me the creeps.

Hobbling through the main entrance, I heard the headteacher's voice booming out from the hall. "Welcome one and all to this exciting concert. I'd like to introduce you all to our *star* pupil. Faustina is the school's youngest ever head girl," he gushed, smiling dotingly at her.

Head girl, when did that *happen?* a voice screamed inside my head.

The audience clapped as Faustina stood up and took a bow, our fellow pupils cheering and whistling. I kept my hands firmly in my pockets.

"Thank you, Mr Haynes," Faustina said, stepping up to the microphone. "As head girl of this school," she paused as some of her friends let out a 'whoop', "I am delighted to lead this fantastic event that we have planned for a good cause, and for your… enjoyment."

The onlookers applauded again. "Now, we would like you all to join us in singing a special song," Faustina cooed in her treacly voice. "The words are very simple."

She clicked her fingers and three huge words flashed up on the screen behind her: *Volisserum, tibrassimus, dedo.*

I stared wildly around. What could I do? *What could I do?*

"Our choir will sing it first – and then you can all repeat it," Faustina purred into the mic.

That's when it came to me! I staggered clumsily back along the corridor and out of the main door as the music teacher started hammering out notes on the piano. I made for the fire escape, hauling myself up the metal steps. I had to stop to blink back tears – the pain in my ankle was almost overpowering and the stair rail was so cold it burned my hands. But the sound of my classmates starting to sing Faustina's spooky song forced me to keep going.

I dragged myself up to the top of the building until I reached a black box on the wall. I wrenched it open and looked at the rows of switches. Which was the right one?

"Okay, everyone, join in," Faustina's voice boomed from the speakers in the hall.

Without stopping to think for another moment, I flung all the switches into the OFF position.

Everything in the building went black. I heard a huge groan from the direction of the hall as the piano crunched to a stop.

Breathing out, I slumped against the wall. Then there was a rustling sound as first one crow, then another, then another, landed on the stair rail beside me, glaring at me with their harsh beady eyes. "Go away," I shouted at them, but they didn't move. Several more descended on the staircase, and I felt my legs tremble slightly.

A voice sliced through the darkness. "Oh, Jez. Here you are again, causing me trouble." Faustina was at an open window just a foot or so away. She clambered out to join me. "What *am* I going to do with you?"

"Back off," I barked, gritting my teeth. "You're not going to do anything to me, *or* the rest of the town."

"What do you mean?" hissed Faustina.

"I mean your evil plan," I said.

"My *plan*?" snapped Faustina, her eyes narrowing.

"Yes, I know everything," I said, my confidence growing with every word. "I know what you are. But you don't scare me. And I'm not going to let you turn the whole town into horrible creatures like you."

Faustina's face fell. "Horrible creatures?" she gasped.

"Yes, *Chamelia venifica* to be exact,"
I said smugly.

Faustina staggered backwards in shock as
her ragged army of crows took to the sky,
circling overhead, cawing and screeching.
"No," she mumbled. "No, you can't know
that… you *can't*…."

"Well I do!" I replied triumphantly, glad
to have taken her by surprise.

"But you don't understand," she
whimpered.

"I think I understand your little scheme
perfectly," I retorted. "And I intend to stop
you – whatever it takes!"

Chapter 11

The Real Faustina

To my astonishment, Faustina's face crumpled and she suddenly looked like a very small, frightened girl. Wait… were those… *tears*?

I looked on, horrified, as Faustina began to cry, sobs shaking her whole body. I didn't know what to do. I'd never been any good when girls started to cry… but then I reminded myself that Faustina wasn't really a girl. She was a *monster*… wasn't she?

"You're so lucky, Jez," she bleated. "You have it *all*."

"Huh," I replied. "Not since you arrived. You've made my life really miserable."

"But don't you see?" she whimpered. "You had everything I'd ever wanted – a loving family, friends. You don't know what it's been like for me." She gulped a deep breath before starting to weep again.

"What do you mean?" I asked – I couldn't help feeling curious.

She looked up at me, wiping her odd eyes dry. "You're right," she said. "About everything. I am a *Chamelia venifica*. And I *am* hideous… in your eyes at least. You see, the thing is," she sighed heavily. "I'm the very last of my kind – I'm all alone," she said in a small voice. "You wouldn't know what that feels like."

"Actually, I've a fairly good idea now, thanks to *you*," I muttered.

"I'm sorry Jez," Faustina said, and for once she actually sounded genuine. "All I wanted was to belong – to have a family of my own."

"But you've made everyone here like you," I pointed out. "You're the most popular girl in school, and everyone hates me. Isn't that enough?"

"No!" cried Faustina. "They like me for who I *pretend* to be. Look, Jez, the truth is I just want to be normal – to be accepted. I want to be able to be myself!" Faustina transformed instantly. No longer a girl, she was now the creature I'd glimpsed once before – a terrifying skull-like face, sharp pointed nose, her hair ragged feathers. But her eyes continued to stare at me forlornly. "You see," she croaked. "No one would like me like… *this*!"

Below, I could see parents filing out of the dark school building into the car park. I thought about Mum, who would be wondering where I was, and poor Dad, still lying in hospital. I thought about Edson. Anger bubbled in my stomach.

"Look this is all very sad," I snapped. "But you can't just go around forcing people to be your family… turning them into monsters!"

"I had no choice!" Faustina shouted. "I spent years working on a spell to turn humans into Chamelias like me–"

"But that's not *fair*!" I yelled.

"Life's not fair, Jez," Faustina bellowed back. "You've ruined everything!"

We locked eyes, glaring at each other. I was so angry I could hardly–

Then a thought struck me. "Hang on," I said. "You've got a spell to turn humans into Chamelias, right?" I asked.

"Yes, I already said that," Faustina snapped.

"Well then, it's only logical that there should be a way to change *you* into a… a human." I said.

A frown creased Faustina's skeletal brow making her look even scarier. "Hmm, I suppose you might be right," she mused.

"Then, if you were a human, you'd be normal – well, as normal as anyone else," I explained. "Look, I read this book once about a magician. He cast a spell but then wished he hadn't so he said the spell backwards… and everything was fixed."

"So you're saying… *what* exactly?" asked Faustina.

"I'm saying why not try your spell backwards? Maybe it will work," I suggested.

"That's silly," spat Faustina.

"Perhaps," I said. "But do you have a better idea?"

"Well, let's see," Faustina huffed. "*Volisserum, tibrassimus, dedo…* so that would be, o-ded, su-mi-… su-mi-sarr-bit, muress-… muress-ilov…. Nothing happened, it doesn't work!"

"You didn't say it properly!" I hissed, and Faustina glared at me. In her Chamelia form, it was pretty unnerving. "We need to write it down," I said. I searched in my pockets for a piece of paper, and found… the photograph of Great Aunt Venetia. Handing it to Faustina, I mumbled, "Now, all we need is a pen."

"Wait," Faustina cried. "What's this?"

She was staring at the writing and symbols on the back of the old picture. "I've no idea," I admitted. "I can't read it."

"Well, I can – at least some of it…. These symbols here mean spell… magic… transform… argh, I can't read the last one, it's too faded. But it's obviously a spell for something."

Faustina looked up from the paper and our eyes met. "Worth a go?" she whispered.

"You never know," I replied.

"*Cardium, perlussium, velocium,*" Faustina chanted, her voice gentle and melodious. I held my breath. "*Cardium, perlussium, velocium–*"

"What's going on up there?" A voice shouted. "Get down immediately – it's not safe!" I looked down to see Mr Fairclough glaring up at us, hands on hips. A crowd of parents and pupils had gathered too, pointing and murmuring.

"Jez! Is that you? Come down here!" Mum screamed at me.

I was about to shout back when something *very* strange happened. I felt Faustina fling herself at me. At first I thought she was trying to push me off the fire escape… but then I realized she was… *hugging* me.

"Thank you," she whispered. "Oh thank you, Jez!"

"Wh-what?" I floundered.

"I'm glad to see you two have made friends," bellowed Mum. "But you're both grounded. Now get down at *once*!"

From the car park, I heard Edson's voice. "Jez! Come down, mate!" He hadn't called me that for ages.

Faustina released me, turned and started to descend, but as I watched she lost her footing. She slipped and pitched forward down the steep steps.

"*Aaaagh!*" she screamed – and before I could think I threw myself towards her, catching hold of her arm. There were gasps from the crowd in the car park as I dragged her back towards me.

I had no idea Floorcloth could move so fast, but in the next moment he was at the top of the fire escape. "Is she all right?" he demanded. "What happened?"

Faustina opened her eyes and blinked. "Yes, I'm fine. I slipped… and Jez saved me from falling."

Shakily, we all headed down the steps, and to my surprise the crowd in the car park burst into applause. Mum ran up to me. "What on earth were you doing up there?" she shrieked. Then she squashed me into a tight hug.

"Er, Mum," I mumbled through her sleeve. "There's something vibrating in your pocket."

"Ooh, my mobile!" cried Mum, releasing me and pulling out the phone. "Now what do I press… oh yes…. Hello?... Oh, it's the hospital," she explained, then her face split into a giant grin. "He's made a miraculous recovery… You're releasing him tonight! Oh thank you, thank you." she said, before hanging up the phone. "Dad's coming home!"

"That's great," I said as Edson ran up to clap me on the back.

"Wow! That was brilliant, Jez!" he said. "You're a hero."

"He is!" Faustina smiled at me. "My cousin, the hero."

"Let's go home and get warm," said Mum. "Edson, you're welcome to come round for a hot chocolate, dear."

"Thanks Mrs Goodwin."

As we headed for the school gates, Faustina put her arm through mine. I noticed that the smell of rotten eggs no longer hung around her. "You know, I think you ought to have your bedroom back, Jez. It's only fair."

"Nah, keep it," I said. "I don't care about a stupid bedroom as long as I get my friends and family back… and get to play for the football team again."

Faustina blushed and I realized she no longer looked as pale as she once did. Her eyes, once odd, were now both a rather nice shade of blue, flecked with brown. "Thanks Jez," she whispered.
"For everything!"

"No problem," I replied. "After all, that's what families are for!"

THE END

FICTION EXPRESS

THE READERS TAKE CONTROL!

Have you ever wanted to change the course of a plot, change a character's destiny, tell an author what to write next?

Well, now you can!

'My Cousin Faustina' was originally written for the award-winning interactive e-book website Fiction Express.

Fiction Express e-books are published in gripping weekly episodes. At the end of each episode, readers are given voting options to decide where the plot goes next. They vote online and the winning vote is then conveyed to the author who writes the next episode, in real time, according to the readers' most popular choice.

www.fictionexpress.co.uk

WINNER
Education Resources
Award for Innovation

FICTION EXPRESS

TALK TO THE AUTHORS

TThe Fiction Express website features a blog where readers can interact with the authors while they are writing. An exciting and unique opportunity!

FANTASTIC TEACHER RESOURCES

Each weekly Fiction Express episode comes with a PDF of teacher resources packed with ideas to extend the text.

"The teaching resources are fab and easily fill a whole week of literacy lessons!"
Rachel Humphries, teacher at Westacre Middle School

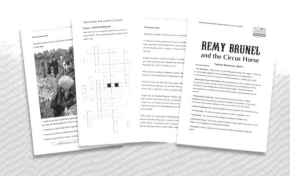

FICTI●N EXPRESS

The School for Supervillains
by Louie Stowell

Mandrake DeVille is on her way to St Luthor's School for Supervillains, where a single act of kindness lands you in the detention pit, while, on the other hand, bullying is positively encouraged. Mandrake is the daughter of billionaire supervillains, with budding superpowers of her own, so in theory, she should thrive at the school. There's just one snag: she secretly wants to be a superhero. Can she possibly succeed?

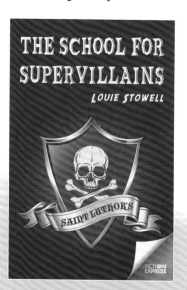

ISBN 978-1-783-22458-6

FICTI●N EXPRESS

Drama Club
by Marie-Louise Jensen

A group of friends are involved in their local youth drama club at a small city theatre. When their leader, the charismatic Mr Beaven, announces he wants to put on a major production at the end of the summer holidays, the cast is very excited.

Amidst rivalry, hopes and disappointments, will there be more drama on or off the stage?

DRAMA CLUB
MARIE-LOUISE JENSEN

ISBN 978-1-783-22457-9

About the Author

Bea Davenport is a former newspaper and BBC journalist whose debut novel for children, *The Serpent House*, was published by Curious Fox in June 2014.

She started writing stories at the age of around eight, but they were all very bad versions of her favourite Enid Blyton adventure tales.

Journalism was her perfect job because it meant meeting new people every day and hearing their extraordinary stories. But then she took a creative writing course and became a published crime fiction and historical fantasy author.

Now she teaches groups of children and adults everything she knows about writing – and she still loves meeting people and hearing their amazing stories.